# MIST
## *of the*
# WESTING WIND

## BOOK ONE

**Books illustrated by Tim Davis**
*Pocket Change*
*Grandpa's Gizmos*
*The Cranky Blue Crab*


**Books written and illustrated by Tim Davis**
*Tales from Dust River Gulch*
*Mice of the Herring Bone*
*Mice of the Nine Lives*
*Mice of the Seven Seas*
*Mice of the Westing Wind, Book I*

# MICE
## *of the*
# WESTING WIND

## BOOK ONE

A two-book sequel to *Mice of the Seven Seas*

Written and Illustrated by

## TIM DAVIS

**journey forth**®

Greenville, South Carolina

**Library of Congress Cataloging-in-Publication Data**

Davis,Tim, 1957-
    Mice of the Westing Wind / written and illustrated by Tim Davis.
        p.    cm.
    "Book one; a two-book sequel to Mice of the Seven Seas."
    Summary: Charles and Oliver help Admiral Winchester with his
plan to recapture the pirate sea dogs who have escaped from prison.
    ISBN 1-57924-065-8
    [1. Pirates—Fiction. 2. Mice—Fiction. 3. Dogs—Fiction. 4.
Cats—Fiction. 5. Castaways—Fiction. 6. Islands—Fiction.]
I. Title.
PZ7.D3179Mk 1998
[Fic]—dc21
                                                    98-14559
                                                        CIP
                                                         AC

# Mice of the Westing Wind, Book I

Edited by Debbie L. Parker
Page design by Duane A. Nichols

Cover and illustrations by Tim Davis

© 1998 by BJU Press
Greenville, South Carolina 29614
JourneyForth Books is a division of BJU Press

Printed in the United States of America

ISBN 978-1-57924-065-3

20  19  18  17  16  15  14  13  12  11  10  9  8  7  6  5  4

*To all my friends*
*at Journey Books*
*and Bob Jones University Press*

The **MICE** series so far:

*Mice of the Herring Bone*
Charles and Oliver risk their lives
to rescue the Queen's treasure
from a crew of scruffy, bad-tempered
pirate sea dogs.

*Mice of the Nine Lives*
Oliver is a hero! He thinks of a plan
to set Admiral Winchester free
from the clutches of the terrible Captain Crag.

*Mice of the Seven Seas*
Charles and Oliver join forces
with some amazing penguins,
and together they ambush the pirates
who are threatening Her Majesty's ship.

A **Westing Wind** blows toward the West.

# Contents

1. Her Majesty's Mice . . . . . . . . . . . 1

2. To the Tower . . . . . . . . . . . . . . 15

3. The Great Escape . . . . . . . . . . . 25

4. In a Fog . . . . . . . . . . . . . . . . 41

5. A Motley Crew . . . . . . . . . . . . 47

6. Caught! . . . . . . . . . . . . . . . . 59

7. Mutiny Brewing . . . . . . . . . . . 67

8. Land Ho! . . . . . . . . . . . . . . . 81

9. In the Dark . . . . . . . . . . . . . . 95

10. Up in the Air . . . . . . . . . . . . 103

## Chapter One
# Her Majesty's Mice

Oliver set down his cup of tea and patted his round belly. He looked at Charles.

"A delicious dinner, wasn't it, old chap? Those cheese bits are the best!"

He glanced out the window. The London street seemed darker than usual, he thought. It was a good night for two mice to be inside swapping sea stories.

"Charles," Oliver said, "we certainly have had more than our share of sea adventures."

"Yes," Charles agreed. "Do you remember the time . . . " And he began another tale of wind and waves, of pirates and treasure.

Their stories quickly tumbled into a playful word game they called "Her Majesty's Ship."

"Her Majesty's ship is an *admiral's ship*," said Charles.

"Her Majesty's ship is a *beautiful ship*," returned Oliver.

"Her Majesty's ship is a *cat-filled ship*."

"Her Majesty's ship is a *dog-stolen ship!*" Oliver laughed at his own wit.

"Her Majesty's ship is *England's ship!*" Charles saluted.

"Her Majesty's ship is a tub of *flea-bitten, mangy, pirate sea-dog scoundrels!*"

The two mice laughed so hard that they could not continue the game.

Charles sighed. "I can tell you're glad those days are all behind us!"

"Most certainly," said Oliver. "Most certainly indeed! What a relief to know that Captain Crag and his sea dogs are all securely in prison! I sleep better at night, now."

"But what great adventures we had," said Charles.

"Don't wish them on us again!" said Oliver. "Perhaps you've forgotten how many times we nearly . . . "

*THUMP, THUMP.*

"Who could be knocking on our door so late?" Charles asked. He scurried up the door frame and loosened the latch. "Come in."

"Thank you, my good mice," said Admiral Winchester. He stepped through the doorway. "Sorry to make my visit so late. But as they say, 'Better late than never!' Ha, ha!"

"Admiral!" cried both mice.

"How very good to see you," said Charles.

"Yes," said Oliver. "We were just talking about you . . . and Crag."

The Admiral's smile faded. "Yes, uh, I'm afraid I have some unpleasant news about Captain Crag and his crew." He pulled at his whiskers. "Perhaps we'd better talk."

He dragged a cat-sized stool over to the wooden counter and sat down on it. Now the mice could speak with him face to face.

"Simply put," began Admiral Winchester, "they've escaped."

"What?"

"Escaped?"

"A most unfortunate situation to be sure," said the Admiral. "That parrot of theirs stole the cell key from one of the guards."

"Barnacle!" Oliver nodded at Charles. They knew that bird well. Too well!

"Her Majesty is quite distressed," said the Admiral.

"And so am I," said Oliver. "We don't live in a guarded castle!"

"Those sea dogs think they have a score to settle with us," said Charles.

"Do not worry about your safety *here*," the Admiral said. "Crag and his crew stole a ship and headed out to sea."

"*Her Majesty's ship is a dog-stolen ship,*" Oliver mumbled to himself.

"What?"

"Oh, nothing," said Oliver.

"Anyway," said Admiral Winchester, "we presume they will continue their pirating ways. They'll go to some island hideout in the Cattibean Sea, no doubt. But I have some good news—we recaptured two of Crag's crew before the rest escaped to sea."

"Oh, really?" said Charles.

"Yes, the first mate, Big Tom. And that peg-legged pirate . . . um, what was his name?"

"O'Grady," replied the mice together.

"That's it—O'Grady," said the Admiral. "Those two scoundrels are securely imprisoned at the Tower now."

"The Tower?" said Charles. "No one's ever escaped from there, have they, Admiral?"

"Quite right, my good mouse," answered the Admiral. He scratched his chin. "At least . . . not yet."

"What do you mean, 'not yet'?" Oliver's whiskers twitched with suspicion.

Admiral Winchester frowned. "Er, that brings me to the business at hand. I have come with a personal invitation from the Queen. Her Majesty wishes you to help bring *all* the sea dogs back to England to face their proper punishment."

"Oh, dear me!" said Oliver.

"Patience, Oliver." Charles patted his friend's broad back. "Let's hear the plan. How *could* Tom and O'Grady escape from such a fortress as the Tower? . . . Unless they were *allowed* to escape for some reason?"

Admiral Winchester smiled. "Ah, Charles, you always seem to be a step ahead of me."

"You mean you're going to let Big Tom and O'Grady go free?" Oliver asked.

"Not without a tail," said the cat. He winked. "A tail that will lead us to the sea-dogs' hideout. Or should I say . . . *two* tails."

"And just what sort of *tails* do you have in mind?" asked Oliver.

"Why, the tails of two noble English mice would be perfect," said the Admiral. "Are you agreed?"

Oliver and Charles looked at each other.

Charles began to pace up and down the counter. "So the Queen would like us to follow those two sea dogs from the Tower . . . "

" . . . To their island hideaway, full of Captain Crag and all his crew," Oliver finished.

"And then what?" Charles asked. "Tie them up and float them all back to England?"

"No, my dear chap!" Admiral Winchester laughed. "Do you remember Mr. Calico, the brave first mate of the *Nine Lives*? He and I, with the rest of our crew, will follow your trail to the pirates' hideout. We'll stay out of sight."

The Admiral stroked his whiskers, looking well pleased with this plan. "We'll take those sea dogs by surprise and deliver them back to Her Majesty's just punishment."

Wish we could stay out of the whole thing, Oliver thought.

11

"What about Tom and O'Grady?" Oliver asked. "Couldn't you just find out from them where the hideout is? No need to let them out of prison at all."

"Oliver, my good mouse, these are *sea dogs!*" said the Admiral. "They are loyal to Crag. As loyal as I . . . and *you*—are to the Queen! They'll tell us nothing, unless it be a lie."

Charles looked at Oliver. Oliver looked at Charles.

"*Her Majesty's ship is England's ship.*" Charles gave Oliver a firm salute.

"You're right, Charles." Oliver saluted back. "For Her Majesty—"

"—and for England—" interrupted Charles. He stood at attention like a soldier.

Oliver joined him, drawing his chubby body up to full height. "We'll do our loyal duty!"

Charles said, "Tell the Queen that we'll gladly follow those sea dogs to the end of the Seven Seas!" His voice grew louder. "We'll recover that ship! We'll—we'll bring those pirates to justice!"

"You don't need to get carried away," Oliver whispered.

"Excellent! Excellent, my good mice!" Admiral Winchester shook the mice's paws so hard that their feet bounced on the wooden counter. "I shall see you then, tomorrow at three. We will supply you with provisions." He paused, looking mysterious. "And we'll tell you about your part in the plan."

The Admiral marched to the door and stepped out into the night with a laugh. "When the cat's aweigh, the mice stalk prey! Ha, ha! Well, cheerio!"

"See you tomorrow, Admiral."

"When the cat's *aweigh*? What did he mean by that?" Oliver asked.

"Seaman's term," said Charles. "It means to haul up the anchor and set out to sea." He looked into his teacup. "More tea, old chap?"

"Certainly," said Oliver. Then he sighed. "This may be our last cup of good English tea for a long, long time."

## Chapter Two
# To the Tower

The next afternoon, Oliver and Charles met with Admiral Winchester and his first mate, Mr. Calico. They discussed provisions, trail markers, and plans.

"You must be very careful on this assignment," said the Admiral. "I fear there will be many dangerous situations."

The mice knew the dangers of being stowaways on a pirate ship. After all, they'd been caught on the *Herring Bone* and almost eaten alive. The thought of that ship filled with sea dogs still gave Oliver the chills.

"Mr. Calico has added some extra precautions to the plan and to your equipment," Admiral Winchester told them.

"This vest—does it have a cork lining?" Oliver asked curiously.

"Aye," replied Mr. Calico. "It'll keep you afloat—just in case you find yourself overboard."

Charles peered through a tiny spyglass. "Amazing optics for such a small telescope, Mr. Calico."

"And it'll fit that secret pocket inside your coat," Mr. Calico said.

"Excellent!" said Charles. "It seems that you've thought of everything."

17

"We can only hope so," said the first mate. He carefully measured out a long piece of slow-burning fuse. "We mustn't forget this—for your floating markers. Just take a piece of fuse, push it into a cork, light it, and throw it out to sea behind the ship. Don't worry. It burns even when it's wet—makes a pink light. We should see it before the dawn breaks."

"Thank you," said Oliver. "We certainly *do* want you to follow us!"

"Aye," replied Mr. Calico, "that we will!"

"Everything is in place at the Tower," Admiral Winchester said. "The guard has been instructed to drop his key just outside the cell. That should give those two sea dogs the opportunity to escape. If for any reason they fail in that attempt, remember Plan B."

"Plan B?" Oliver scratched his head.

"The window," Charles reminded him.

"Aye," said Mr. Calico. "We've changed the window bars to tin. And we've left a rope in the mattress so they can climb down the outside wall."

"Oh, yes," replied Oliver. "*That* Plan B."

Late afternoon shadows slanted in dark lines across the streets.

"Time to go to the Tower and put this plan into action, mates," the Admiral said. "Let's pin the tail to the doggie—*sea* doggie, that is! Ha, ha!"

But no one else laughed.

By the time they arrived at the Tower, a cold, swirling fog had settled over everything. Tall white stone walls rose from the mist.

Oliver stayed close to Charles as they walked over the drawbridge and up to the massive front gate. Guards on either side saluted as they entered.

"I suppose they know what we're here to do," Oliver whispered to Charles.

"Most certainly," he replied. "Otherwise those sea dogs could never get out of this place."

"I guess you're right," said Oliver. "It'll be hard enough as it is!"

"And remember, Oliver, we've got to follow them."

They hurried after the cats as they marched up the Tower's long staircase.

Charles and Oliver struggled to climb the stone steps as they wound around and around.

Oliver held a hand up to his head. "I'm getting dizzy," he said.

At last they reached the top. They stopped in front of a wooden door with a small barred window and an iron lock. The Admiral took out his key, unlocked the door, and swung it open.

*Creeeeak.*

"Here's your cell, my good mice," the Admiral said. "Enjoy your privacy while you can. In a few moments, two sea-dog prisoners will be transferred to this cell."

"We're already acquainted," said Oliver. "I think we'll just keep to ourselves."

"Indeed!" Mr. Calico and the Admiral laughed.

"You'll find a proper hiding place behind the bed." Admiral Winchester stepped over to the straw mattress and pointed to two small holes in the stone wall. "There—two fine mouse holes, with a passage between them."

"You *have* thought of everything," said Charles.

"Perhaps more than you realize," answered the Admiral. "Well then, we must be leaving. A safe trip to you both. Rest assured that Mr. Calico and I will follow your marked trail most carefully. Cheerio, my friends."

"Good-bye!"

The two cats and the two mice gave hearty pawshakes all around. Then the cats stepped out of the cell, and Admiral Winchester locked the heavy door behind them.

Oliver and Charles listened to their footsteps tap down the stone steps until all was quiet.

"You know," whispered Oliver, "a pirate ship might be welcome, compared to this place."

"If all goes as planned, we'll be there soon enough," answered Charles.

## Chapter Three
# The Great Escape

Oliver began to chew nervously on his whiskers. Then he stopped. "I think I hear something," he said.

Charles nodded. "Footsteps."

*Tap, tap, tap, ker-thonk, tap, tap. Tap, tap, tap, ker-thonk, tap, tap.*

The footsteps—and the sound of jingling keys and grumbling voices—came closer.

"Why'd ya have to wake us up in the middle of the night? One cell's as good as another when yer dreamin' of bein' elsewhere."

"Captain's orders."

"Ahhh. Quit yer complaining, O'Grady. At least we gets a little air up 'ere. That dungeon's as damp as the hold of a leaky ship."

"Aww. Poor Tom, did ya get a fungus between yer big toes?" O'Grady laughed, a high-pitched cackle.

"Naw—you musta got some b'tween yer ears."

*Ker-thonk.*

"Ooowww! Get offa my foot!"

"Settle down, you two, before we dig another dungeon just for you." The guard's keys rattled in the lock.

Oliver and Charles scampered into their holes. From here they could still see perfectly well.

"Enjoy your stay," the guard said. He unlocked the door and pushed the two sea dogs inside. "There's a nice view of the moat out the window."

He pulled out another ring of keys and took the handcuffs off the two pirates. "See you two in the morning."

*Slam. Clicka-clink.* He closed and locked the door.

*Tap, tap.*

*Kah-ting.*

Oliver nudged Charles. That was the sound of a key dropping from the guard's pocket.

*Tap, tap. Tap, tap. Tap, tap.* The guard's steps faded down the stairs.

Big Tom stood looking out the barred window on the door. Before long, he made the discovery.

"Well, shiver me timbers!" he said. "There's a key just outside the door. The guard musta dropped it."

O'Grady's peg leg tapped with excitement.

"Cut that out," growled Tom. "You'll rouse the guards. We gotta get that key before they finds out it's missin'."

"What if it ain't the right one?"

"Let's just get it and find out, ya flea-brain." Tom glanced around the cell. "This here'll do." He pulled a long splint of wood from a ceiling beam.

He poked it between the bars toward the key. "Aargh, almost! Can't get my arm far enough. Here, O'Grady, you got no meat on yer arms. You try. I'll hold ya up ta the window."

O'Grady climbed onto Tom's thick neck and reached the wooden splint toward the key.

Oliver clamped a hand over his mouth to keep from giggling at the sight of the pirate standing on top of the other dog's shoulders. Charles grinned, too.

"Oooh, come to O'Grady, sweet key," the sea dog said. "C'mon now . . . Got it!!"

O'Grady hooked the key as if it were a fish and drew it slowly back towards him.

"C'mon." O'Grady breathed heavily. "C'mon." The key dangled on the end of the stick.

31

Suddenly, O'Grady's peg leg shook with excitement. It poked Tom in the eye.

"Aaaargh!" Tom dropped O'Grady, who dropped the stick, which dropped the key—

*Kah-ting, kah-tinka, ting, ting, ting.*

The key bounced down several steps and landed well out of reach.

The two pirates insulted each other in typical sea-dog terms. Charles looked at Oliver.

Oliver rolled his eyes in disgust. "It looks like this might take a while."

"Well, there's still the outside window," said Charles. "I hope it won't be too long until they find out the bars are weak."

"I'll pull the rope a little way out of the straw," said Oliver. "Maybe they'll get the hint."

"Good idea, Oliver."

Before long, O'Grady came upon the rope. "Why lookie 'ere, Tom. Somebody left a rope in the straw."

"Ha! Must of been left from balin' hay or somethin'." Tom chuckled. "We could climb out the window with that rope. I'll test the window bars!" The big dog grabbed the window bars and easily bent them apart.

"Har, har, this 'ere's as good as a key," the burly pirate said with a laugh. Then he poked his head out the window. "That moat's pretty far down there. Ooooh, hope that rope's good and strong."

"It'll do," said O'Grady. "It'll do!"

The pirates tied the rope securely to the iron bars of the door, stretched it across the little room, and flung it through the outside window. O'Grady climbed out the window first.

"Shiver me timbers, Tom," said O'Grady, "it's quite a drop!" His peg leg rattled on the window ledge.

"Shhh!" said Tom. He gave him a shove. "Just get movin'!"

O'Grady edged his way along the rope and down the stone wall. Tom climbed up on the window ledge to follow.

O'Grady's voice came from outside. "The rope don't reach far enough."

"Maybe we can swing over that moat to the outside wall," said Tom.

The rope scratched roughly on the window ledge as O'Grady swung himself back and forth.

Big Tom slid down to join him.

As soon as the sea dogs had gone, Charles and Oliver left their hiding place. They climbed up to the window ledge and peered down.

The rope swung back and forth, back and forth. Over the moat and back to the wall, over the moat and back to the wall. Each time, the pirates got a little closer to the outside wall.

But the rope was rubbing on the window ledge. It was wearing thinner and thinner . . .

*Snap!*

*"Whoooah!"*

*Splash. SPLASH.*

Tom and O'Grady thrashed around in the moat below, swimming noisily toward the outside wall.

"It's a good thing the guards are supposed to ignore them," said Oliver.

"They'd never get out of here otherwise," said Charles.

The two mice squeezed under the cell door, scampered down the winding stairs, and ran out through the front gate.

A guard called, "Over in the moat by the back tower."

"Yes," said Charles, "we know."

Oliver ran beside Charles across the drawbridge and along the outside wall. They paused in a clump of tall grass. Fog swirled around them. Oliver couldn't see much, but soon he heard the sound of dripping water. It came from just above them on top of the wall.

"Drop me that rope, Tom."

Tom, muttering under his breath, yanked O'Grady up out of the moat to the top of the outside wall. The soaking sea dog tried to stand, lost his balance, and fell over the wall, accidentally hooking the rope around Tom's ankle on the way down.

*Thud.* "Oooof."

*THUMP.* "Aaaaargh!"

The two pirates landed in a heap just in front of Charles and Oliver. Quickly the mice ducked into the tall grass.

"C'mon, O'Grady, pull up yer anchor," growled Tom. "Let's get outta here!"

The two dripping sea dogs set out for the shipyards, snarling at each other. Charles and Oliver ran silently after them into the night.

Finally they reached the shipyards, but more fog had rolled in. It hung like a thick gray curtain between them and the pirate sea dogs.

"We've lost—them!" said Oliver, panting from their long run.

## Chapter Four
# In a Fog

The two mice stopped, peering in all directions. Just ahead, the docked ships groaned against their wooden moorings. Tall masts rose like a gray forest in the fog.

"We'll never find them in this cloud," Oliver said.

"Wait," whispered Charles. He cupped his hand around his ear to hear above the waves lapping at the docks.

*Ker-thonk, ker-thonk.*

"This way," said Charles. They plunged into the billowing fog again. They passed ship after ship but found no sign of the sea dogs.

"I can't—run much—longer," panted Oliver.

"There's a light!" said Charles.

They crept toward the glow of a lantern.

Oliver could see the dark silhouette of a sinister-looking cat. The cat was talking to two sea dogs—or was it three?

"We've—found them," Oliver sighed.

"Shhh," said Charles.

The sailors ahead spoke in hushed and low tones, but before long Oliver could make out snatches of the conversation. It sounded as if the cat and his first mate, a dog, were striking a deal with Tom and O'Grady.

"Payment? Why—uh—you'll have a share o' pirate treasure!" said Tom.

"*What* treasure?" asked O'Grady. "Er, yes—what *treasure* it be! Eh, Tom?"

"Oh,—er, aye mates."

"And ya wants passage to the Cattibean, ya say—eh?" The cat slouched over his lantern. He wore a large captain's hat, and a black patch covered one eye. "What do ya say, Willy? Yer an old sea dog. Can we trust these mutts ta keep their side o' the deal—eh?"

Willy circled around Tom and O'Grady, sniffing. "They smells like our kind . . . I says we take 'em along."

"Then it's a deal, mates," said the cat. "You stay outta sight. The rest 'o the crew'll be reportin' for duty at dawn. The *Westing Wind* sets sail with the first mornin' breeze."

Everyone shook paws. Tom and O'Grady stepped onboard the ship and disappeared below deck.

Oliver peered from behind a barrel. He whispered, "Looks like those sea dogs will fit in just fine with *that* captain and first mate."

"No respectable captain would take them into his crew," said Charles.

"Oh, the company we keep," sighed Oliver. "I can hardly wait to see the rest of the crew!"

"I'm sure we'll see them soon enough." Charles motioned Oliver to follow him onto the ship. "Oh, just a minute, Oliver." He stopped at a wooden post in front of the ship and pulled a scarlet rope out of his pocket. He tied the rope securely to the post.

"There!" he said. "We mustn't forget to leave a trail."

"Right-oh," said Oliver. "I'd quite forgotten."

"Now we can get onboard."

"And find a hiding place," added Oliver. "Let's get as far away from this dreadful crew as possible!"

## Chapter Five
# A Motley Crew

Early the next morning, the sound of footsteps awakened Oliver.

He nudged his friend. "Charles, wake up!"

Charles sat upright and listened. "Sounds like the crew's loading up and coming on-board." He stretched. "Let's sneak up and get a good look at our traveling companions."

The two mice carefully climbed up through the hold. Above them they could hear the sound of rolling barrels, scuffling feet, and grumbling voices.

"Lend a hand 'ere!"

"Ugh, ummmph."

*Thud*—the sound of a wooden crate dropping on deck.

Charles and Oliver crept silently up to the main deck and climbed into a coil of rope. The fog lifted, revealing the deck in the dim light of early morning. From their hiding place, Oliver could see the crew reporting for duty. They were a sorry-looking lot—a combination of dirty dogs and unkempt cats.

"Phew," said Oliver. "What is that smell?"

Willy, the first mate, walked by. He was a scraggly-haired terrier, and he left an unusual odor in the air around him.

Charles wrinkled his nose. "I wonder when he last saw a bathtub."

"At least we won't have to worry about him sneaking up on us," said Oliver.

Two Siamese cats came up the ramp, rolling a barrel between them.

"They look like twins," whispered Oliver. "Both with bad tempers."

Behind them, carrying a wooden crate close to his face, came another sailor.

*Ker-thonk, ker-thonk.* Oliver had no doubt who that was, even with the strange hat that shaded the sailor's face.

"Better stay away from that one," whispered Charles.

Behind O'Grady followed a collection of mongrels and misfits. There was a toothless black cat; a drooling, wrinkled hound dog; an untamed Australian dingo; and even a wildcat. The last two crew members to board the ship sent shivers up Oliver's spine: two large rats.

The two mice ducked lower into the coiled rope to avoid those black, shifting eyes.

"I don't like the looks of them," whispered Oliver.

"Nor do I," said Charles. "We'd best be very careful with them prowling around the ship."

The door to the captain's cabin opened. Out stepped the sinister-looking cat. A large, feathered hat kept his face in shadow, but Oliver could still see his black eye patch. The captain strutted out onto the deck and called for the crew's attention.

"Listen 'ere," he began. "The breeze is pickin' up. Soon we'll set sail fer the balmy Cattibean Sea. Hurry up an' load the stuff—there'll be no slackers on this ship! We cast off within the hour. To the work, mates!"

Oliver looked at Charles. "I do believe that if Crag were a cat, he would be this very captain!"

"Perhaps so," said Charles. "We'd best stay out of his way too."

"Not to mention those rats," said Oliver.

Together they ran quietly back down into the ship's lower deck.

The ship's hold was dark and damp. Oliver shivered at the thought that this was to be their home for days—until the ship reached the Cattibean Sea.

As the trip dragged on, Oliver and Charles took care to remain well hidden. They spent their days sleeping in the stale air of the ship's hold, and they spent their nights tasting tidbits from the ship's cargo.

Each night, when the crew had gone to their bunks, Charles dropped one of Mr. Calico's floating trail markers off the back of the ship. The lighted fuse glowed a bright pink, sparkling all through the night in the midst of the waves.

One evening, Charles lifted his nose and sniffed the warm air. "We must be getting close to the Cattibean Sea."

"Do you think the *Nine Lives* has seen our markers?" asked Oliver. "I guess it's more important than ever to leave a trail for them."

"That's for certain," agreed Charles. "Did you get another piece of cork for tonight's trail marker?"

"Yes," said Oliver, "but I can't find any more matches."

Charles took the cork and pushed the fuse into it. "We'll have to light it on a lantern."

"I don't like the sound of that," said Oliver. "What if somebody sees us?"

"We'll just have to be careful. I think the Captain keeps a lantern burning in his cabin."

"Oh dear me! Do we have to go in *there?*" asked Oliver.

"It's probably safer than a lantern that's out in the open," said Charles. "Besides, he should be sound asleep."

"I just hope those rats aren't on watch tonight!" said Oliver.

They climbed up toward the deck and passed through the crew's sleeping quarters.

All manner of horrible snores and whistles filled the air.

"This place gives me the *willies,*" whispered Oliver. He trembled a bit.

55

"Speaking of which . . . " Charles held his nose as they passed Willy's bunk.

The mice scurried up the ladder and slipped into the shadows on the main deck. It was a clear, warm night, and a full moon shone in the sky. Oliver stayed close behind Charles. They ran softly towards the Captain's cabin, keeping to the shadow of the rail.

Charles stopped suddenly, still in the shadows. They stood just a few feet from the Captain's cabin. In front of them was a lighted part of the deck. They'd have to race across it and squeeze under the Captain's door.

"This will have to be quick," warned Charles. "I think I saw one of those rats on watch up in the rigging."

"And that moonlight's awfully bright tonight," said Oliver.

"All right, on the count of three," Charles whispered. "One . . . two . . . three!"

They sprinted for the door. Charles slipped under easily, but it was a tight squeeze for Oliver. Charles had to yank on his friend's paw to pull him through.

"Ouch," squeaked Oliver.

"Shhhh! Quiet, Oliver." Charles motioned for him to follow.

"Wait," whispered Oliver. "I'm still stuck!" "It's my tail!" Oliver turned and yanked at it with his paw.

Suddenly, his tail yanked back.

## Chapter Six
# Caught!

High-pitched laughter came from the other side of the door.

Oliver froze as the door opened partway. A large rat stood there in the moonlight. He had a firm grasp on Oliver's tail.

"Going somewhere?" The rat chattered with glee.

The door opened farther. Two rats! thought Oliver.

The second rat clenched a sword between his teeth. He muttered from one side of his mouth, "You're coming with us, mates!"

Charles took a step backwards and threw the cork at the rat who held Oliver's tail. It hit him square in the nose. Then Charles grabbed Oliver's paw and snatched him away from the rat's grasp. "C'mon, Oliver!"

They dashed into the Captain's cabin.

The rats raced after the two mice. They chased Charles and Oliver around table legs and chairs, under the bed, then up onto it. Oliver and Charles ran onto the blanket. Then suddenly—*whoosh! Thump, thump.*

The rats had pulled the blanket off the bed and captured the mice in a tangle of bedding.

"What's this?" The Captain sat up in his bed and shook himself. "Merton! . . . Nelson!" he exclaimed. "What's going on?"

61

He scowled. "I hope you have good cause ta yank off my blanket in the middle of the night!"

Merton narrowed his dark eyes. "Aye, Captain, that we do."

The other rat untangled Oliver and Charles from the blanket and held each one firmly by the ear. "Stowaways, Cap'n," he announced.

"Hmmm. Good work, Nelson," purred the Captain. "I'll deal with them from here on. You two get back to yer watch."

Merton and Nelson looked disappointed. "Aye, aye, Cap'n," Merton said. They went back out and shut the door behind them.

The captain dropped the dazed mice onto his table and strutted in circles around it.

He stroked his chin and muttered, "Stowaways, eh?"

Oliver's heart pounded like a drum. That cat might snatch them up at any minute and pop them down his throat. He watched the Captain and shook with fear.

Suddenly the cat bent over and glared at them, eyeball to eyeball. Oliver could feel his hot breath as he spoke. "You two look familiar ta me . . . Do I look familiar ta you?" He pulled off his black eye patch so quickly that Oliver had to close his eyes.

Before Oliver could open his eyes again, Charles said, "Is it? Yes! Captain Tabby—of the *Seven Seas*?"

"Captain Tabby!" squeaked Oliver. "But what's . . . "

"Let me explain," whispered the captain. "I'm in on the plan."

"Her Majesty's plan?" asked Charles.

"Yes, but quiet now, my good mice," Captain Tabby whispered. "There are too many ears on this ship! No one must hear what I'm about to tell you. I lured Big Tom and O'Grady onto my ship by posing as a rather unsavory character."

"Oh yes, *quite* unsavory," said Oliver.

The cat's whiskers twitched. "Thank you." He continued. "Unfortunately, I attracted many other unsavory characters along with them. Now my crew is quite undependable. In fact, Tom and O'Grady have become popular with many of them. That whole group seems untrustworthy and dangerous . . . and so I must continue my role with great caution."

The Captain stopped, listening a moment. "I advise you to do the same."

Charles and Oliver exchanged a nervous glance. They both nodded.

"No one must suspect . . . "

*THUMP, THUMP, THUMP.*

Captain Tabby glanced toward his door. He motioned the mice to climb out his window. "One minute, mate," he called.

Oliver and Charles waved to him, then scurried out onto the window ledge. They carefully inched along, around the outside of the cabin, and Oliver tried not to think about the dark sea below. Once they were safely around, they quickly slid down from the rail.

Then they ran silently from shadow to shadow across the deck.

When they had arrived safely back in the hold, Oliver heaved a sigh. "Oh, how I hope that's the last we see of those rats!"

"Or they see of us," said Charles.

## Chapter Seven
# Mutiny Brewing

After tossing and turning through the night, Oliver sat up suddenly. He gazed at the gray morning light that filtered down through the open hatch. He turned to Charles, who was already awake. "Someone's coming," he whispered.

*Tap, tap, ker-thonk, pitter-pat, pitter-pat.*

Charles and Oliver slipped into the darkness of a pile of ropes, keeping close watch on the hatch.

"Are ya sure ya seen two *mice* last night, Merton?" It was Big Tom's voice.

"Aye, me an' Nelson both—almost had 'em ta ourselves too."

"Then the Captain woke up an' took 'em."

"Ooohh, I hates mice." That was O'Grady's voice. *Rat-a-tatta-a-tat-tat tatta-tat.* His peg leg rattled on the boards just above. "Specially *those* two," he muttered.

"What two?" asked Merton's deep voice.

Tom growled. "Ah, O'Grady's still fussin' about those cat-lovin' varmints back in London who done us in time after time."

"Aye," added O'Grady. "Charles an' Oliver!"

"*Oliver?*" asked Merton. "Nelson, weren't that the name we heard one call the other?"

"Aye," replied Nelson. "I believe yer right."

"What?" barked the sea dogs together.

Down in the hold, Oliver grabbed for Charles's paw.

"An' what'd the captain do with them mice," hissed O'Grady, his peg leg tapping again.

"Aye, thar's the curious thing," said Merton. "We thought we heard 'em just talkin' together."

"Oh, reeeeally now," Tom said with a growl. "So what do ya say ta that? Our dear Captain being friendly with them little mice!"

"Ya can't trust *none* a them cats!" snapped O'Grady.

"Maybe yer right, fer once," said Tom. "Maybe it's time this here ship was under a *dog's* command!"

*Ratta-tatta-rat-tatta-rat-tatta-tatta.* O'Grady's peg leg danced on the deck.

"Aye, Tom, ya'd make a fine captain," cackled O'Grady. The rats joined in, and they chattered excitedly.

Soon the pirates and rats left. Charles and Oliver sighed together.

"We've got to go and warn Captain Tabby!" Charles said. "And we've got to do it right away!"

"Oh, dear," squeaked Oliver. "The crew is probably all up and about by now."

"I know," said Charles. "We'll just have to be extra careful!"

Once again they ran up to the lower deck. They crept along the inside wall of the hull.

Then they both dove under a wide cannon mount as two dogs shuffled by.

"Tom says we can take the ship," whispered one dog to the other.

"I'm all fer that," agreed the other. "I'm not takin' my orders from a cat—no more!"

Oliver followed Charles to the main deck. He tried to look in every direction at once. The other dogs were muttering among themselves too.

"Word travels fast!" whispered Oliver.

"Too fast," agreed Charles. "We've got to find the Captain."

But the deck buzzed with activity. The crew was busy doing the morning chores.

The dogs were trimming the sails, mending the rigging, and swabbing the deck.

The suds on deck were so slippery that Oliver fell flat on his face more than once. No one seemed to notice them. But where was Captain Tabby? The two mice slipped and slid to the back of the ship, near the Captain's cabin.

"I'm not squeezing under that door again," whispered Oliver.

"Let's sneak along the rail and go up onto his back window ledge," said Charles.

The mice darted past another crew member who was swabbing the deck. They pulled themselves up onto the outside rail and carefully inched along. Gray clouds gathered overhead. Foaming gray blue waves churned noisily below.

"Don't look down, Oliver."

They continued until the rail met the window ledge at the back of the ship. Voices drifted out from inside. Charles and Oliver peered around the edge of the window frame and into the cabin. There stood Big Tom and O'Grady . . . and Captain Tabby. His mouth was gagged with a black bandanna, and his hands were tied behind his back.

Tom grinned. "Ere's how it'll be, Cap'n—er, let's just call ya *mate . . .* "

O'Grady cackled with glee, his peg leg tapping wildly.

"We'll step out yer door together," continued Tom. "An' I'll announce the change o' command. Then you'll see what happens.

Every cat will be bound up by a sea dog before one of 'em can say, 'meow'!"

"Aye, aye, Cap'n Tom," said O'Grady.

"Oh, dear me," sighed Charles. He turned to Oliver. "Oh! Look out—behind you!"

Oliver leaped sideways just in time to escape Merton's claws. He and Charles took another frightened leap and ended up right in front of the Captain's window.

"Thar they are!" barked O'Grady from inside the cabin. He rushed toward them.

Nelson dropped onto the ledge in front of them and waited, snarling.

Oliver and Charles skidded to a stop. There was no escape.

"The sea!" shouted Charles.

Together they jumped off the window ledge—just missing the paws of O'Grady, Nelson, and Merton.

*Splash! Splash!*

*Gurgle, glug, glug, gurgle.*

Together they plunged underwater. They twirled like tops in the foamy wake of the *Westing Wind*.

Oliver felt dizzy. He flipped upside-down, then right-side up. Under the surface—then bobbing on the waves. He heard gurgling, then rumbling thunder. He reached for Charles's arm . . . Everything became gray, and then he heard and saw nothing at all.

Rain poured steadily down, rousing Oliver to his senses. Charles swam beside him, clutching his arm. Oliver blinked and sneezed.

"Oliver," said Charles. "I'm so glad you're awake again!"

Oliver raised his head and shook himself. That seemed to clear his head a bit. "Where are we, Charles?"

"Floating along somewhere—who knows *where?*—in the Cattibean Sea."

"How long have we been out here in the water?"

"Quite some time. Two, maybe three hours," said Charles. "At least the rain's letting up a little."

"I guess these cork-lined vests are proving quite useful."

"Indeed! Many thanks to Mr. Calico."

"I just hope we're floating towards someplace that has food."

"Oliver," said Charles, "you must be feeling better."

Before long, the rain became a fine mist. Then the clouds lifted from the sea. A dark outline began to take shape ahead of them.

"Look Charles! What's that?"

"Looks like an island!"

## Chapter Eight
# Land Ho!

The sun broke through the clouds, and Oliver could see the island more clearly. Its emerald bay was rimmed with white sand. Palm trees waved a welcome on the shore. Out of the island's center rose a great mountain, clothed in green and topped with fluffy clouds. A steaming waterfall spilled from the mountain and trickled back into the bay.

"It's beautiful," said Oliver.

"Right-oh!" said Charles. "It seems we're being swept right into an island paradise!"

A strong current carried them now, and they bobbed on top of the sparkling waves.

Soon they reached shallow water. Oliver could see bottom now—and what a sight it was!

He poked his head under the surface and came back up. "Look, Charles, an underwater flower garden!"

"A coral reef," Charles said. He chuckled. "Astounding—just look at all the colors!"

Oliver ducked underwater again. Some corals were green, like giant leafy clovers. Some were white, like little smokestacks. Some were yellow, like dyed lace. All around were what looked like pink fingers and red pincushions and stubby purple pots. Brightly colored fish swam past, and Oliver thought they could have been painted by a circus clown.

He came up for another breath of air. "That's astounding!" he repeated.

A school of small fish darted past the reef, flashing silver in the sun. They passed so closely that some of their fins tickled Oliver's whiskers. Seconds later, three sharp-toothed barracuda sped underneath them.

Charles and Oliver swirled round and round in circles.

"Let's hurry up and get to shore!" said Charles. Oliver had already started swimming that way as fast as he could.

Before long, the two mice washed up onto the wet, white sand.

"Charles—" panted Oliver, "I think I've seen enough of that reef."

They dragged themselves across the hot beach. They squeezed out of their wet clothes and spread them out to dry in the hot sun.

Then they searched for a spot of shade on the beach, curled up, and fell fast asleep.

Oliver woke up . . . or was he *dreaming?* He rubbed his eyes—yes, his clothes *were* walking along the beach!

"Hey!—stop!" he called.

The clothes sprang up into the air. From under them, spindly crabs scurried for cover. They scuttled under rocks or dug down into the beach, and sand flew everywhere.

The noise roused Charles from his long nap.

"Did you see that?" Oliver asked.

"Most peculiar!" answered Charles. "It seems this island has some surprises in store for us."

"I think I've had enough surprises for a while." Oliver gathered up his clothes. "Let's go find something to eat—I'm starved!"

They dressed quickly and headed into the forest to look for some supper. They found a great variety of nuts and berries to nibble on. Many of the fruits had delicious and unusual flavors.

The forest also supplied a feast for their eyes. What an abundance of wildflowers, Oliver thought. Colorful butterflies flitted about like petals flying from one blossom to another. Tiny hummingbirds sipped nectar from the flowers, but they sped into hiding at the sight of their wide-eyed visitors.

Oliver and Charles strolled under the trees until finally the shadows grew long.

A chorus of tree frogs rose from the twilight and replaced the forest's bird song. Oliver heard a rustling in the tall grass. He stopped and stared at the grass. His whiskers trembled.

"We'd better find a safe place for the night," said Charles.

Oliver heartily agreed. "But where?" he asked.

"I wish I knew."

*zzzzzzzzzzzzzzzzzzzzz. Thwap.*

"What was that?" asked Oliver.

Charles shrugged. "Let's walk a little faster."

*ZZZZzzzzzzzZZZZZZzzzzzz.*

The humming noise grew louder and louder. *Thwap. Thwap. Thwap.*

Soon a cloud of mosquitoes buzzed around them.

Charles and Oliver slapped at the mosquitoes. Half-running, half-dancing, they hurried under a low-hanging branch. Oliver tripped and landed with his face in the grass.

*Thwaap!* A slimy tongue picked a mosquito
clean off his ear. The tongue snapped back into
the mouth of a black-and-orange tree frog. He
smiled. He took another insect off Charles's
tail.

"Better go," croaked the frog. "Eat you up."

Oliver stared at the slimy frog in horror.

"Not me," croaked the frog, "them." He shot out his tongue and gathered up two more mosquitoes from Oliver's back.

"Go where?" said Charles. He waved the bugs away again.

"Up hill," croaked the frog. "At clearing—" *Thwap.* He ate another mosquito.

"Go down—short tree." The frog swung away and occupied his tongue with a dozen more mosquitoes.

The mice turned and ran up the hill, still slapping at the mosquitoes.

"Go down—short tree?" repeated Oliver. "What does *that* mean?"

"Who knows? But it's worth a try!"

Just ahead, on the brow of the hill, Oliver saw the clearing. There *was* a short-looking palm tree! It was so short that its leaves seemed to dip under the ground.

He and Charles dashed the rest of the way up the hill.

"Whooaa!" yelled Charles. They had nearly run straight into a gaping hole in the ground. The "short" tree grew up out of it—but it wasn't really short at all. Its trunk dropped out of sight, deep into a dark hole below.

"That frog *did* say, 'go down,' " squeaked Oliver, still waving away mosquitoes.

Charles looked down into the hole and then he looked up. "Let me stand on your shoulders, Oliver. I think I can reach this palm leaf."

"All right, but . . . " Oliver hoped Charles knew what he was doing. He let his friend climb up on his back.

"When I grab this palm leaf, our weight should swing us down to the trunk."

Charles stretched his arms high overhead. "Ugh . . . got it—step over the edge, Oliver, and hold onto my feet!"

"Here goes . . . " said Oliver. "But I can't even see the bottom!"

The palm bowed down with their weight, but not as far as Charles had hoped. The mice hung in the air, dangling halfway between the tree trunk and the edge of the hole.

"Dear me!" said Charles, peering into the darkness below. "Maybe if we . . . "

" . . . *if we,*" his voice echoed back.

Oliver strained to see the bottom. "Sounds pretty deep."

" . . . *pretty deep.*"

"*Eeeee! Eeeee!*" A high-pitched squeak sounded from below. Then more squeaks. More and more squeaks. A mighty rushing sound came toward them out of the darkness.

Suddenly hundreds of flapping wings surrounded them.

"Bats!" yelled Charles. "Hold on tight, Oliver!"

**Chapter Nine**
# In the Dark

"Are you all right, Oliver?"

"I think so."

They still dangled over the dark hole. Charles was holding on to the palm leaf, and Oliver was holding on to Charles.

"Well, then, what was I saying before we were interrupted?" asked Charles. "Maybe if we swing back and forth a bit, this palm will bend a little farther."

"And we can climb down the trunk?"

"Right-ho! Go ahead and start swinging, Oliver. My arms are getting tired."

Oliver did exactly that. Back and forth, back and forth, back and . . .

*Kerrrrack—swiiiishhhh—BONK!* The palm bent suddenly, sending Oliver swinging into the trunk, nose first.

"Ouch!"

"Splendid!" Charles grabbed the rough bark. "Sorry about your nose, my good fellow."

They climbed down the tree trunk. Oliver had to stop and rub his nose a few times.

"At least there are no mosquitoes down here," said Charles. "Nice and cool too."

" . . . *cool too,*" repeated the echo.

"But a little dark for my taste," said Oliver.

" . . . *my taste.*"

Dark it was. Now only moonlight cast its faint light into the cave. When the mice finally reached the bottom, they could see only a few dead palm leaves at their feet. And all they could hear was the slow sound of dripping water.

"It seems safe enough down here."

" . . . *down here,*" said Charles's echo.

"But when are those bats coming back?" Oliver wondered.

"Eeen the morning," came a voice from the cave wall.

Oliver shook himself. "Since when do echoes answer questions?" he asked.

"Hee, heee, I'm not an echo," answered the voice, "but I like them."

Oliver's heart started beating so loudly that he thought it was making an echo itself.

"Who's there?" called Charles.

"*Who's there*?" said his echo.

"Who eez *there?*" asked the voice. Its echo was interrupted by a high-pitched squeak and the sound of flapping wings.

"We're loyal subjects of Her Majesty, the Queen," Charles boldly replied. "And we're on a mission to bring Captain Crag and his pirates back to prison where they belong!"

"So pleeezed to meeet you." A gray-haired bat emerged from the darkness and landed before the two mice.

Charles and Oliver jumped back.

"Pleeeze don't bee afraid," answered the bat. "I meeean no harm. My name eez Emeeelio."

"I'm Charles." He extended his paw in greeting. "This is my good friend, Oliver."

"Pleeezed to meeet you," said Oliver.

"Forgeeeve mee for asking," said Emilio, "but why do you theeenk you weeel find seeea dogs in my cave?"

"I'm afraid that's a rather long story," said Oliver.

"I'm all eeeears," said the bat.

One question led to another, until Charles and Oliver had told their whole story to Emilio. The bat listened. He scratched his gray head, and then he carefully refolded his wings.

"Wee have seeen seeea dogs on *theees* island," he said, squinting his tiny eyes.

"You have?" said the mice together.

"Some yeeeears ago," continued the bat. "They trampled through thee forest, set big fires on thee beeeach, and smoked out thee mosqueeetoes for a weeeeek! Made a reeeeeal mess of theeengs!"

"Sorry to hear that," said Oliver, scratching an itchy mosquito bite.

"We'd be pleeezed to help you capture them if wee can."

"Thank you for that most generous offer," replied Charles. After a pause he said, "Perhaps you could help us find a way off this island."

"Eeezier to come than to go," Emilio scratched his chin. "The seeea welcomes ships *into* thee bay, but very deeeeficult going *out.*"

"We don't even *have* a ship," said Oliver.

"Eeeeven more deeeeficult, then." The bat scratched his ear, refolded his wings, then scratched his chin again. "I tell you what. Hop on my back, and I'll geeeve you a tour of thee island. Maybee you can seeee some way off."

"Well . . . " said Oliver.

"Thank you," said Charles. "Let's go."

Charles and Oliver climbed onto Emilio's back. The gray bat slowly unfolded his wings. He jumped off the cave floor and flew up past the palm leaves, up high into the starry sky.

## Chapter 10
# Up in the Air

First Emilio turned toward the bay where Charles and Oliver had washed ashore.

He looked down at the waves and Charles and Oliver looked too. "You seeee how the current pushes eeeenland, into thee bay," Emilio said.

"That's how we floated in," said Charles. "But aren't there any other bays in the island?"

"You'll seee," answered the bat. He snapped up a mosquito in midair.

He flew higher, in a wide circle, and Oliver studied the whole coastline of the island.

All he could see was the ocean pounding against steep cliffs or crashing against rocks.

"There eez a saying about our island," said Emilio. "You are welcome to come, but forbeedden to go."

"I can see why," said Charles. "There's no way for us to get off!"

"Most ships dare not to land," said the bat. "And those who do . . . " He shook his head. "Only thee strongest sailors can beeeat the current and get away."

"We're hardly strong sailors," murmured Oliver.

"Courage, old chap," said Charles. "We'll think of something."

"Maybee you can stay," said the bat.

Oliver almost smiled at the thought of no more sea dogs. How nice that would be, he thought.

"You're most gracious, Emilio," said Charles, "but we have an important job to do."

"Indeed," agreed Oliver. "But we're stuck on this island, Charles! How can we ever do our job if we can't get away?"

Charles bit his lip. "I wish I knew," he said with a sigh.

Emilio smiled. "Let meee fly you over thee mountain. It weel give you a lift. Hee, heee."

The bat turned toward the center of the island. He flapped higher and higher until they rose as high as the flattened peak of the great mountain ahead.

"There's a warm wind out tonight," said Charles.

"Hee, hee. That eez thee mountain," said the bat, flapping harder. "You weel seee!"

Just ahead, the steaming waterfall spilled out of the mountainside, sparkling in the moonlight. Its warm spray wafted toward them, and droplets trickled down Oliver's whiskers.

"Hot running water!" yelled Charles over the water's roar.

Emilio flapped up toward the edge of the mountaintop. As they flew closer, Oliver could see the great mountain's wide-open mouth. It bubbled with hot water.

"Wow!" cried Charles. "It's gigantic!"

"And hot!" said Oliver.

"That it eeez!" called Emilio. "A slow-boileeng volcano—but seeeing it eez not the best part . . . feeeeling it eez! Hold on tightleee!"

At that moment, they passed over the lip of the crater. A sudden rush of hot air below them lifted Emilio and his passengers up like an arrow shot high into the night sky.

"Wheeeeeeeeeeeee!" cried the bat.

Oliver felt as if his stomach had fallen down to his toes.

The bat laughed. "It's beeeen a while seeence I dared to do theees." They rose higher and higher.

Oliver opened his eyes. He took a deep breath and peeked down at the island.

109

It seemed no bigger than the top of a barrel. "Are we going back now?" he whispered.

"Oh yes, my good friends," answered the bat. "What goes up, neeeeds to come down. Heee heee!" He turned and began a long spiral away from the stars and down to the island.

"Perhaps we *are* forbidden to leave," Oliver whispered in Charles's ear. He thought about the powerful current that kept them there.

"You could be right," said Charles.

Emilio fluttered through the clearing and down into the mouth of the cave.

"I hope you enjoyed thee tour," he said.

Oliver gulped. "It was unforgettable!"

"Quite so," said Charles. "But I'm afraid I still don't see how we'll be able to get off this island."

"I'm so sorreee," said Emilio. "It eez veery deefficult indeeeed." The bat shook his head. "Pleeeze, my good friends, be our guests heere in the cave. Have yourselves some sleeep . . . Good night."

"Thank you," said Charles. "And thank you for welcoming us to your island."

"Looks like we may be staying for a while," said Oliver with a sigh.

Silently the two mice pulled together some dried leaves for a mattress, and then they settled down to rest.

But Oliver couldn't sleep. "Did you . . . did you happen to think of anything yet?"

"Not yet," said Charles. "I sort of hoped that Emilio . . . "

"So did I," said Oliver sadly. "I'm afraid we've failed Her Majesty, Charles. We didn't capture those sea dogs. And we left Captain Tabby in terrible danger."

Charles put a paw on Oliver's plump shoulder. "You talk as if we're finished. Not *us*—the heroic Mice of the *Herring Bone*, owners of the Queen's Medal of Courage! Cheer up, old chap. We've only just begun!"

Will Charles and Oliver ever get off
this strange and beautiful island?

And if they do, will they manage to
outwit crafty Captain Crag once again?

Don't miss . . .
*Mice of the Westing Wind, Book Two.*